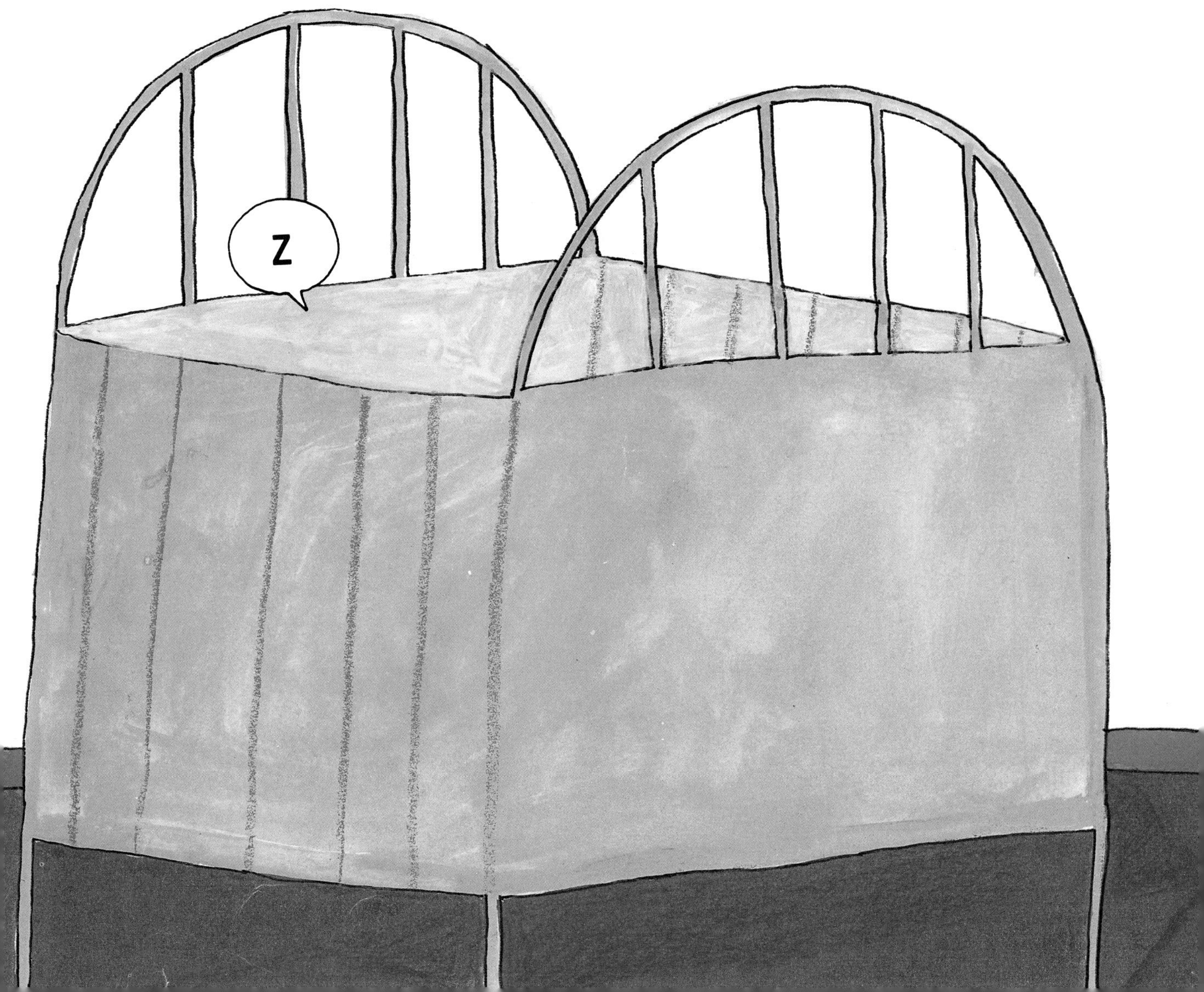
z

JONATHAN FRANKLIN

DON'T WAKE THE BABY

Farrar · Straus · Giroux / New York

For Ari, Clara, and Linda

Library of Congress catalog card number: 90—83184
Published simultaneously in Canada by
HarperCollins*CanadaLtd*
Color separations by Imago Publishing, Ltd.
Printed and bound by Horowitz/Rae Manufacturers
Designed by Martha Rago
First edition, 1991

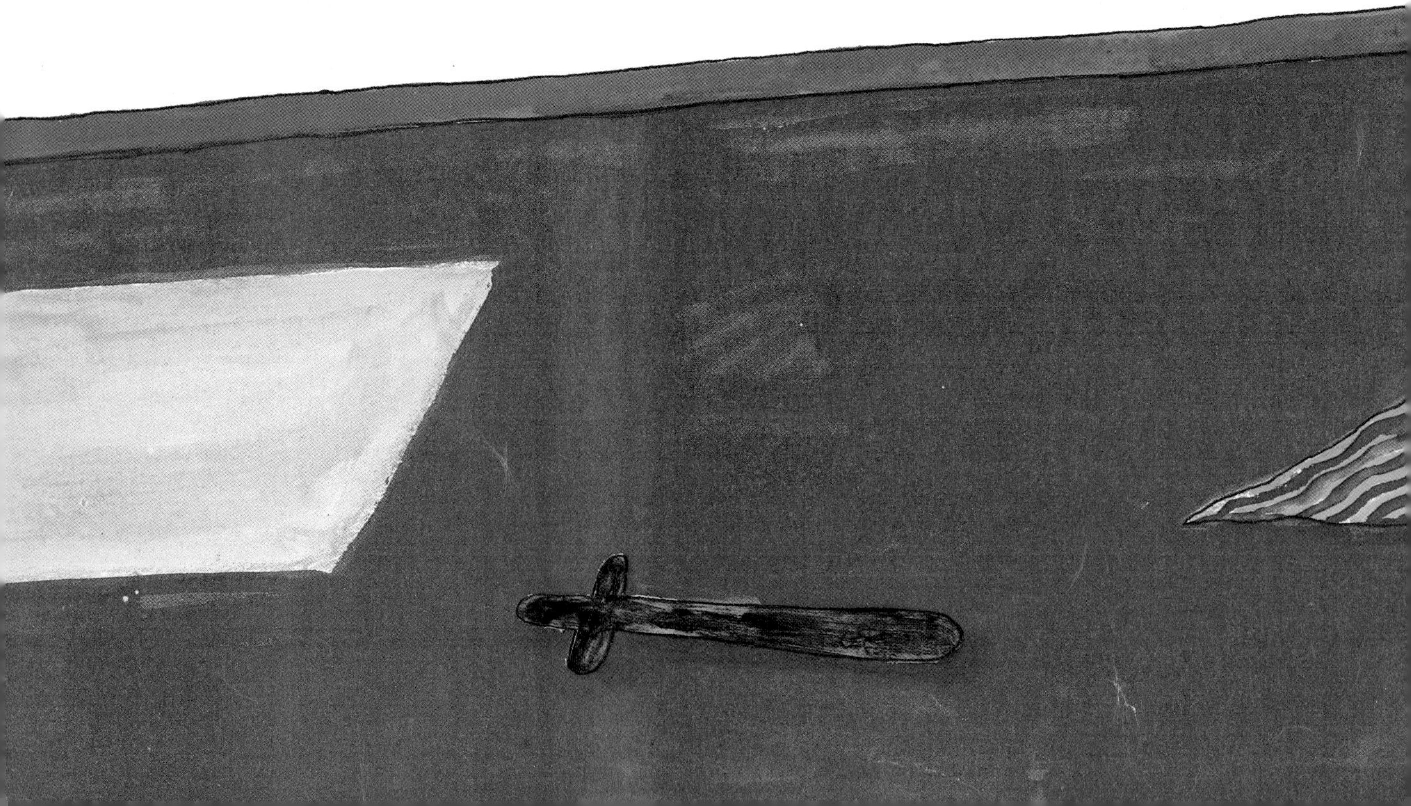

Tickle
Tickle
Z

Don’t wake the baby, Marvin.
z

Z

What
are you doing?

Z

I hear noise.
Z

Z

You'd better not be doing what I think you're doing.
Z

Z

I'm warning you.
z

Coochie coochie coo
Z

Not another peep.
z

Z

One more sound
and I'm coming in.
Z

Z

MARVIN!
Z

WORLD CHAMPION
Z

Z
FIVE FOUR THREE TWO ONE BLAST OFF!

Captain Marvin

That's better.

Z

Z
z

It's too quiet down there, Marvin.

Z
z

WAH!

Uh-oh